Amy
the Amethyst
Fairy

To Enid and Miriam,
my fairy grandmothers

Special thanks to
Narinder Dhami

No part of this work may be reproduced, stored in a retrieval system, or transmitted in any form or by any means, electronic, mechanical, photocopying, recording, or otherwise, without written permission of the publisher. For information regarding permission, write to Rainbow Magic Limited, c/o HIT Entertainment, 830 South Greenville Avenue, Allen, TX 75002-3320.

ISBN-13: 978-0-439-93532-6
ISBN-10: 0-439--93532-6

12 11 10 9 8 7 6 5   10 11 12 13 14/0
Printed in the U.S.A.   40
First Scholastic printing, September 2007

Amy
the Amethyst
Fairy

by Daisy Meadows

SCHOLASTIC INC.

New York   Toronto   London   Auckland
Sydney   Mexico City   New Delhi   Hong Kong

The Fairyland Palace

Adventure Playground

Tippington Manor

Tippington Town

The Tall Toy Store

Fountain

Twisty Tree

Jack Frost's Ice Castle

Pegasus

Cherrywell Village

FANCY DRESS

Rachel's House

Buttercup Farm

Scarecrow

Chestnut Tree

By frosty magic I cast away
These seven jewels with their fiery rays,
So their magic powers will not be felt
And my icy castle shall not melt.

The fairies may search high and low
To find the gems and take them home.
But I will send my goblin guards
To make the fairies' mission hard.

Contents

Ready for Adventure

Welcome to Tippington Manor

"Kirsty, we're here!" Rachel Walker announced, looking out of the car window. She pointed at a large sign on the wall that read WELCOME TO TIPPINGTON MANOR.

Kirsty Tate, Rachel's best friend, was peering up at the cloudy sky. "I hope it doesn't rain," she said. Then the house

caught her eye. "Oh, look, Rachel, there's the house! Isn't it beautiful?"

At the bottom of the long gravel driveway stood Tippington Manor. It was a huge Victorian house with an enormous wooden door, rows of tall windows, and old red bricks covered with ivy. The house was surrounded by gardens full of flowers and trees, their autumn leaves glowing in shades of red and gold.

"Look over there, Kirsty," Rachel said as Mr. Walker turned the car into the parking lot. "A playground!"

Kirsty looked where Rachel was pointing and spotted the playground on a hill behind the house. She could see some tire swings, a silver slide, and what looked like a big wooden tree house in the middle, built around a tall oak tree.

"Isn't it great?" Kirsty whispered to Rachel as they climbed out of the car. "The fairies would love that tree house!"

Rachel grinned and nodded. She and Kirsty knew just what the fairies would like, because they were friends with them! Whenever there was trouble in Fairyland, the two girls tried to help.

The fairies' biggest problem was Jack Frost. He had recently stolen the seven magic jewels from the Queen of Fairyland's crown. Because the gems controlled much of the magic in Fairyland, greedy Jack Frost had wanted them for himself. But when the glowing heat and light of the jewels had started to melt his ice castle, Jack Frost had angrily tossed them out into the human world.

The fairies had asked Rachel and Kirsty to help them find the jewels and return them to the queen's crown. But Jack Frost had sent his mean goblins to guard the gems, which made getting them back a whole lot harder.

"I know where you two want to go first!" Mrs. Walker laughed as Kirsty and Rachel stared eagerly at the tree house. "Let's all go in together. Then you can explore the playground while your dad and I look at the flowers. They have a famous orchid collection here."

"Orchids are Dad's favorite flowers," Rachel told Kirsty, rolling her eyes. "He's crazy about them!"

Mr. Walker laughed. "They're very beautiful and unusual," he explained. "But a lot of them are tropical, so they need to be kept in greenhouses."

A wooden sign pointed toward the orchid houses. The girls followed Mr. and Mrs. Walker down the twisting path around the beautiful gardens.

The path took them to the bottom of a hill. There they found three large glass greenhouses filled with orchids, and a little gift shop selling plants.

"You girls have fun on the playground," Mr. Walker said with a smile. "We'll meet you back here in an hour."

Rachel and Kirsty waved and headed toward the playground.

"I wonder when we'll find the next

magic jewel," Kirsty said thoughtfully. "We only have a few more days before I have to go home."

"Don't worry, we'll find them all," Rachel said in a determined voice. "I know we will."

At that moment, the sun broke through the gray clouds. The cold, crisp air immediately seemed a little warmer. "That's better!" Rachel said, smiling in the sunshine.

Just then, the girls reached the playground. "There's no one else here," Kirsty said happily, looking around.

"That's great!" Rachel laughed. "It's like our very own playground!"

Aside from the swings, there was a big slide, a sandbox, and a maze made of

tires and rope ladders. But right in
the middle of the playground was the
biggest and best tree house the girls had
ever seen!

It was built around the trunk of a huge
old oak, and was painted green with
little round windows.

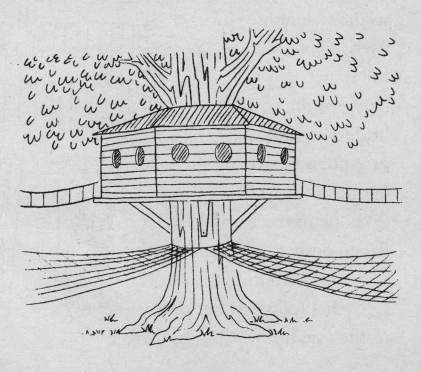

There were four other trees
around the oak, each with
wooden bridges attached to
them. The bridges made a circle
around the central tree trunk,
while two more bridges led
from outer trees directly
to the tree house
itself. There were
safety nets
between the
bridges to make
sure nobody would
get hurt if they fell.

"Look at the tree house!"
Kirsty gasped. "It's amazing!
Let's climb up to it!"

Rachel followed Kirsty over
to the tree house. "Look, there's

only one way to get up there," she said, pointing to a ladder attached to one of the outer trees. "You go first, Kirsty." Kirsty began to climb the ladder, with Rachel close behind. When they reached the top, they were near one of the two bridges that led right to the tree house itself. "This is great," Kirsty said as they walked across the bridge, holding on to the rope railings. "And we have it all to ourselves!"

When they reached the tree house, Rachel suddenly felt a sharp tug at the back of her head. It was almost like somebody had pulled her hair. She stopped and turned around to see that the pink ribbon from her ponytail was dangling from a branch overhead.

"Hang on, Kirsty!" she called to her friend, who was already inside the tree house. "The ribbon from my ponytail just came out. It got caught on a branch as we were crossing the bridge."

Kirsty turned to look. "Quick, go grab it before the breeze blows it away," she said.

Rachel was just about to step back onto the bridge when something strange happened. The bridge began to shimmer and flicker, and for a moment parts of it seemed to disappear!

Rachel and Kirsty blinked in surprise. But when they looked again, the bridge had reappeared, looking just as normal as ever.

"Did you see that, Kirsty?" Rachel gasped.

"Yes, I did!" replied Kirsty, unable to believe her eyes. "Do you think — ?"

But before she could say anything else, the bridge began to flicker out of sight again. The girls rubbed their eyes in disbelief, but this time the bridge didn't come back. It had completely vanished!

Now You See It, Now You Don't!

"It's gone!" Rachel said in amazement. She peered out across the safety net, but there was no sign of the bridge they had just crossed. "Do you think it could be fairy magic?"

Kirsty smiled. "Maybe one of the magic jewels is nearby," she suggested.

"Doesn't one of them control appearing and disappearing magic?"

"Yes," Rachel agreed excitedly. "Amy's amethyst! Maybe it's somewhere in the tree house."

"If it is, we'll have to be on the lookout for goblins," Kirsty reminded her.

Rachel nodded. "I don't know how I'm going to get my hair ribbon back," she sighed. Her ribbon was still dangling from the tree branch. "I can't reach it without the bridge." Suddenly, her eyes widened.

"Kirsty, how are we going to get down

again? That bridge led back to the
ladder!"

"Don't worry," Kirsty replied. She
turned and pointed to the
bridge that stretched
away in the opposite
direction. "After we
search the tree house,
we'll go that way.
Then we can walk
around the outer
circle of bridges back
to the ladder again."

Rachel grinned, looking relieved.
"Right! Good idea."

"Rachel! Kirsty!" A silvery voice
interrupted them.

The girls spun around at the sound of
the sweet, clear voice. A tiny fairy was

swinging from Rachel's ribbon and
waving at them! She wore dark purple
pants, a lilac top, and dainty lilac shoes.
Her wand was a glittering purple, and
she wore her curly brown hair tied up in
a ponytail, decorated with three purple
flowers.

"It's Amy the Amethyst Fairy!" Kirsty gasped.

Amy freed Rachel's ribbon from the branch. Then, smiling widely, she floated gracefully down toward the girls. The pink ribbon streamed out behind her like a banner.

"I'm so glad you're here!" she said, landing lightly on Kirsty's shoulder. "I need your help."

"Thank you, Amy," Rachel said gratefully, taking the ribbon from the tiny fairy. "Do you think your amethyst is nearby?"

Amy nodded. "I'm sure it is," she replied. "I can feel that it's not far away. Now I just need to find its hiding place."

"We saw that bridge disappear," explained Kirsty, pointing at the spot where the bridge had been. "One minute it was there, and then it was gone!"

Amy looked very excited. "I knew I  could feel the amethyst working its magic!" she cried, dancing up and down on Kirsty's shoulder. "Have you seen any goblins?"

"Not yet," Kirsty replied. "We were just about to search the tree house for your amethyst."

"Let's get started!" said Amy, fluttering toward the tree house door.

Kirsty and Rachel followed her inside. The tree house was big, but there wasn't much inside. The girls saw a few benches, a little wooden table, and the thick trunk of the oak tree growing through the middle of the room. It didn't take Amy and the girls very long to realize that the amethyst wasn't there.

"Oh, dear," Amy said with a sigh, her wings drooping. "I was so sure we'd find it in here."

"Don't worry, Amy," Kirsty comforted her. "We can search all the bridges and the trees, too. Speaking of bridges, I wonder if the one that vanished has come back yet?"

While Kirsty glanced out the window and saw that the bridge had still not reappeared, Rachel looked out the opposite window to make sure that nothing else had vanished. But just then a flash of light caught her eye. Was she imagining it, or had she just seen a purple sparkle in the branches of one of the trees?

Rachel blinked and stared. There it was again! "Kirsty! Amy!" she cried. "I can see something shining in that tree — and it's purple!"

Kirsty and Amy rushed over to the window. Like Rachel, they could both see something purple, glittering in the sunshine.

"It must be my amethyst!" Amy gasped, twirling around in the air with excitement.

"Let's go look," Kirsty said, heading to
the tree house door.

The two girls hurried outside with Amy
flying alongside them. The tree where
Rachel had spotted the amethyst was
at the end of the other bridge. It
connected the tree house to the outer
circle of trees.

"I hope this bridge doesn't disappear,"
Kirsty said anxiously as they hurried
across it.

"Girls, I can see my amethyst!" Amy cried joyfully. "It's up there, on that crooked branch."

The girls looked up where Amy was pointing. Sure enough, they could see a large, purple jewel sitting on the branch. It glowed and winked with a rich lilac light in the sunshine.

"Oh, it's beautiful!" Kirsty breathed.

Suddenly, Rachel stopped in her tracks.

"What's that noise?" she asked, looking around.

Ha-ha-ha! Hee-hee-hee!

Rachel grabbed Kirsty's arm. "Look!" she cried, pointing up ahead.

A grinning goblin wearing thick gloves was perched on the branch above the jewel. As the girls and Amy watched in horror, he leaned down and reached out to grab the amethyst.

Amethyst Alert!

Before the girls or Amy could do
anything, the goblin grabbed the
amethyst and held it high above his head.

"The amethyst is mine!" he cackled,
dancing gleefully up and down on the
branch. "Hooray!"

"We have to get it back!" Amy gasped,
swooping forward. "Quickly, girls!"

Rachel and Kirsty dashed after her. But before they reached the tree, the goblin raced off around the outer circle of bridges. When he got to the next tree, he stopped and glanced back over his shoulder.

"You can't catch me!" he sneered, sticking his tongue out at the girls. Then he took off again, running around the tree house.

"Kirsty!" Rachel panted as they chased him. "He's heading toward the ladder to the ground. He's going to escape!"

"Oh, no!" Kirsty groaned, seeing that Rachel was right.

The goblin looked very pleased with himself as he ran toward the last bridge and the ladder. But all of a sudden, the last bridge began to blur and flicker. Just before the goblin reached it, it vanished into thin air!

"Ohhh!" The goblin cried, surprised. He tried to stop but was going so fast that he skidded right into the tree where the bridge had been attached. "Ouch!" he grumbled, rubbing his nose. "That hurt!"

"We've got him!" Rachel yelled triumphantly. "That tree doesn't have a bridge over to the tree house. His only way out now is to come back past us."

"Give me back my amethyst!" cried Amy, fluttering toward the goblin with a determined look on her face.

The goblin scowled at her. "No way!"

he yelled. But then he looked around in
confusion. First he gazed at the empty
space where the bridge had been, then he
looked at Amy and the girls, who were
hurrying toward him.

"Over here!" came a yell. Someone
was shouting from the tree house in a
rough, gruff voice!

Amy, Rachel, and
Kirsty turned around
and were dismayed to
see two warty-faced
green goblins leaning
out of the tree house
windows! They were
waving at the goblin
who held the amethyst.

One of them was wearing gloves.

"Over here!" the one with the gloves shrieked. "Throw it to me!"

Amy, Rachel, and Kirsty watched in horror as the goblin with the amethyst drew back his arm and hurled the jewel through the air. The glowing gem went spinning and tumbling toward the tree house. As it passed, branches, ropes, and leaves mysteriously appeared and disappeared, and a glittering trail of purple sparkles crackled in the air.

"Quick!" Rachel shouted. "Back to the
tree house!"

The girls began racing around the circle
of bridges again as the goblin in the
tree house leaned out and caught
the jewel.

He gave a screech of triumph. "I have
the amethyst now!" he yelled gleefully
to the girls. "And you're not getting it back!"

"We have to stop those goblins!" Kirsty
panted.

"There's only one way they can go,"
Rachel replied, stopping as they reached
the bridge that led from the outer
circle back to the tree house. "And it's
this way!"

At that moment, the two
goblins dashed out of
the house, and
Kirsty realized that
Rachel was right.
Because the
other bridge had
disappeared, there
was only one
bridge leading
away from the tree
house now — and she,
Rachel, and Amy were
standing right at the end of it!

The goblins stopped, looking angry when they saw Amy and the girls blocking their path. They began whispering to each other. A moment later, they swung themselves over the edge of the bridge and dropped down onto the safety net below. Then they began clambering across the net toward the ladder.

"Oh, no!" Amy cried. "Those horrible goblins are escaping with my amethyst!"

Kirsty Swings Into Action

Kirsty turned to the little fairy. "Amy, can you make Rachel and me fairy-size?" she asked. "Then we won't have to worry about the bridges appearing and disappearing."

Amy nodded and waved her wand in the air. A shower of lilac-colored sparkles fell softly onto Rachel and Kirsty, turning

them into tiny fairies with shimmering
wings.

"But we're all too small to snag the
amethyst back now," Amy pointed out.
"What are we going to do?"

"We can distract the goblins and keep
them from escaping," Kirsty replied.
"That will give us more time to figure
out how to get the jewel."

"Maybe we can make them drop it,"
suggested Rachel.

"Good idea," Amy agreed.

Kirsty, Rachel, and Amy flew down
and hovered around the goblins' heads.
The first goblin had joined his two
friends, but all three of them were
annoyed because their big feet
kept getting stuck in the
safety net.

"Pesky fairies!"
the one holding
the amethyst
shouted. He
swung wildly
at Rachel, but
missed her by a
lot. "Go away!"

"Help, I'm stuck!" shouted
another. Amy had flown at him, and
he'd fallen over backward. "My feet are
caught in the holes!" he wailed.

The other two goblins ignored him.
They were too busy trying to scramble
across the net toward the ladder.

Amy and the girls fluttered around the
head of the goblin with
the amethyst, doing
their best to make
him drop the jewel.
Unfortunately, he
was clinging to
it tightly.

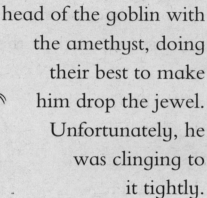

Suddenly, Kirsty
noticed a long, thick rope hanging
down in front of her. She was sure it
hadn't been there before, and realized
that it must have appeared because of
the amethyst's magic. The dangling
rope gave Kirsty an idea, and she
waved at Rachel and Amy.

"Quick! Back to
the tree house!"
she cried, grabbing
the end of the rope
and zooming up into
the air with it.

"But the goblins
are getting away!"
Rachel yelled back.

"I know, so hurry!"
Kirsty insisted. "I
have an idea."

Amy and Rachel
followed Kirsty back to the tree house.
As soon as they landed, Kirsty turned to
Amy. "Can you make us human-size
again?" she asked.

Amy nodded and raised her wand once
more. As soon as the girls were back to

their normal sizes, Kirsty got a firm
grip on the rope. Then, taking a
deep breath, she leaned
backward and swung herself
off the tree house
platform and
out over the
safety net.

"Kirsty, be
careful!"
Rachel and
Amy both cried
anxiously.

As Kirsty flew
through the air,
she saw that the goblins had
almost reached the tree with
the ladder. They were looking
very pleased with

themselves, and they hadn't
noticed her swinging in their
direction. They
laughed and
slapped one
another on
the back. At
the same
time, Kirsty
swung silently
toward the goblin
who held the amethyst.
She knew she had to be
quick, because she'd
only get one chance. As
Kirsty swept past the
goblin, she snatched
the magic amethyst right
out of his gloved hand!

The goblin's eyes almost popped out of his head. He gave a scream of rage. "Give that back!" he roared.

"I don't think so!" Kirsty yelled, clutching the jewel tightly as the rope carried her back toward the tree house and her waiting friends.

As soon as she could reach, Rachel grabbed Kirsty and pulled her safely back onto the platform.

"My amethyst!" Amy cried joyfully, fluttering down to the jewel glowing in Kirsty's hand.

"And look," Rachel said, her eyes wide in amazement. "The bridge is back!"

Kirsty and Amy turned to look. The first bridge to the ladder, which the girls had crossed to reach the tree house in the first place, had now reappeared.

"That means we can get out of here right away," Kirsty said happily, heading across the bridge. "Come on!"

Rachel and Amy followed her. But as they stepped onto the bridge, three very angry goblins appeared at the other end. They were completely blocking the friends' escape!

Trapped!

"We're trapped!" Kirsty gasped, looking around for a way out.

But it was no use. Two of the goblins were running across the bridge toward them, while the other stood guard at the ladder.

"You can't get away!" one goblin yelled. "So give us the amethyst!"

"Never!" Amy cried bravely.

Rachel looked around desperately for
something to help them escape from the
goblins. Suddenly, her eyes fell on
the silver slide on the other side of the
playground. She turned to Amy. "Amy,
could you use your magic to make a
slide appear?" she asked. "Then we could
slide safely down to the ground."

Amy nodded and lifted her wand. A
swirl of lilac sparkles cascaded to
the ground. There was a flash of
purple smoke. Then, between
the safety nets, appeared a
beautiful, shiny slide,
spiraling all the way
down to the ground.

"Great idea,
Rachel!" Kirsty
gasped, clutching the
amethyst tightly and
leaping onto the slide.

"Hurry!" Amy urged
the girls, as she
hovered anxiously
over their heads.
"The goblins are right
behind us!"

Kirsty pushed herself off and Rachel slid down after her. Kirsty found herself whizzing along quickly, her hair streaming out behind her. She landed safely at the bottom and jumped off the slide, just before Rachel reached the bottom.

"Quickly, girls!" Amy flew down and landed on Kirsty's shoulder. "The goblins are coming!"

Rachel and Kirsty began to run beneath the safety nets. But to their dismay, the goblins were already whizzing down the slide!

"Ouch! Ow!" they yelled as they bumped into one another at the bottom. They rolled off onto the grass, picked themselves up, and raced after the girls.

"They're getting closer!" Kirsty panted as she ducked underneath another safety net. "How are we going to get away?"

Amy smiled. "This time I have an idea!" she whispered, raising her eyebrows mischievously.

Rachel and Kirsty watched as Amy first touched the tip of her wand to the magic amethyst, then flew up to touch her wand to the safety net. The disappearing and appearing magic of the amethyst began to work. The knots in the ropes holding up the net began to vanish! Amid a dazzling shower of lilac sparkles, the net slowly came free of its ropes.

As the goblins dashed toward Rachel
and Kirsty, the net began to float
downward. Understanding Amy's plan,
the girls darted out from underneath the
net just in time. Down it came, right on
top of the goblins!

Tangled Goblins

The goblins yelled in anger and struggled to free themselves. But as they flailed, they only got more and more tangled in the net. Soon they were arguing with one another.

"Help!" cried one.

"My nose is stuck!" yelled another.

"Get your foot out of my ear!" shouted the third.

Rachel and Kirsty stood watching them and couldn't help laughing. "Good job, Amy," said Kirsty. "It's going to take forever for them to untangle themselves!"

"And by then my amethyst will be back in Queen Titania's crown," Amy said happily. She touched the tip of her wand to the jewel in Kirsty's hand, releasing a purple sparkle. Then she waved her wand expertly in the air. Another safety net magically appeared to replace the one that held the goblins.

"Now nobody playing in the tree house will fall and get hurt," Amy announced. Kirsty and Rachel watched as she waved her wand over the amethyst one last time and sent it back to Fairyland in a swirl of fiery purple sparkles.

"Thank you so much, girls," Amy went on. She fluttered onto Kirsty's shoulder, and then onto Rachel's, planting soft kisses on their cheeks. "Now the amethyst is back where it belongs, and it's time for me to go home."

"We'd better go, too, Kirsty," said Rachel, glancing at her watch. "It's time to meet Mom and Dad at the greenhouses."

Kirsty smiled at their fairy friend. "Good-bye, Amy."

Amy waved her wand at the girls and zoomed up into the sky. "Good-bye, girls!" she called in her silvery voice. "Don't forget, we're counting on you to find the other magic jewels!"

Kirsty and Rachel nodded and waved, then hurried out of the playground.

"That was fun!" Rachel said with a grin as they ran down the hill. "But I was really afraid the goblins were going to get away with the jewel this time."

"So was I," Kirsty agreed. "Look, there's your mom and dad."

Mr. and Mrs. Walker were just walking out of the greenhouse. The girls raced over to join them.

"What do you have there, Dad?" Rachel asked, noticing that her dad was carrying something very carefully.

"It's an orchid," Mr. Walker replied. He pulled back the tissue paper that was wrapped around the pot. "I bought it in the store. Isn't it beautiful?"

Rachel and Kirsty stared at the exotic-looking purple flower.

"It's exactly the same color as Amy's amethyst!" Kirsty whispered to Rachel with a smile.

"It's beautiful, Dad," Rachel told him, smiling, too.

Mr. and Mrs. Walker carried the orchid over to the car, and Rachel and Kirsty followed.

"So, now we've found our fifth jewel," Kirsty said happily. "Queen Titania's crown is almost complete again!"

"Yes, only two more jewels left to find," Rachel agreed thoughtfully. "I wonder where they could be!"

India, Scarlett, Emily, Chloe, and Amy
all have their jewels back. Can Rachel
and Kirsty help

Sophie
the Sapphire
Fairy?

Wishes in the Air

"I wish this rain would stop," Kirsty Tate said to her friend Rachel Walker as they splashed through the puddles on Main Street. "My sneakers are soaked." She pulled the rainbow-colored umbrella she was holding farther down over their heads.

"Mine, too," Rachel said. "But I'm

glad we came into town today. I got the perfect present for Danny's birthday party next week." She swung the shopping bag she was holding. It contained a bright red turbo-charged squirt gun that Rachel was sure Danny, her six-year-old cousin, would love.

"I wish I was going to be here for his party," said Kirsty, sighing.

"Me, too. I can't believe you're going home tomorrow," Rachel told her. "This week went by so fast."

"Too fast," replied Kirsty. "I just hope we find another jewel today."

The two girls exchanged a look. They shared an incredible secret. They were best friends with the fairies! They'd helped the fairies out lots of times in the past. This time, mean Jack Frost had stolen seven magic jewels from Queen Titania's crown. Rachel and Kirsty had already helped five of the Jewel Fairies get their magic jewels back, but there were still two gems missing — the sapphire that controlled wishing magic and the diamond that controlled flying magic. Rachel and Kirsty had to find them as soon as possible. The fairies' special jewel celebration was supposed to take place the very next day!

RAINBOW magic™

THE PETAL FAIRIES

Keep Fairyland in Bloom!

SCHOLASTIC

www.scholastic.com
www.rainbowmagiconline.com

HiT entertainment

PFAIRIES

There's Magic in Every Series!

The Rainbow Fairies

The Weather Fairies

The Jewel Fairies

The Pet Fairies

The Fun Day Fairies

The Petal Fairies

The Dance Fairies

Read them all!

SPECIAL EDITION

More Rainbow Magic Fun!
Three Stories in One!